D1300866

WORDS

Written and illustrated by

Lora Rozler

WORDS PUBLISHING

WORDS

Written and illustrated by Lora Rozler

Designed by Mauricio Bonifaz

Text and illustrations copyright © 2015 Lora Rozler

ISBN: 978-0-9947576-0-9 (Paperback) • ISBN: 978-0-9947576-1-6 (Hardback)

LIBRARY AND ARCHIVES CANADA CATALOGUING IN PUBLICATION

Library of Congress Control Number: 2015905382

Text is set in Gotham Book

Words Publishing

Published in Canada by
Words Publishing
www.wordspublishing.ca

To Nicole and Shawn,
      I love you beyond words.

To Mauricio Bonifaz,
      my endless gratitude for
            helping me build castles.

                                    - L.R.

There once was a letter alone on a page,

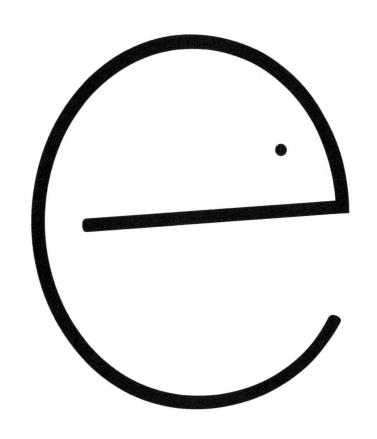

surrounded by a sea of white space.

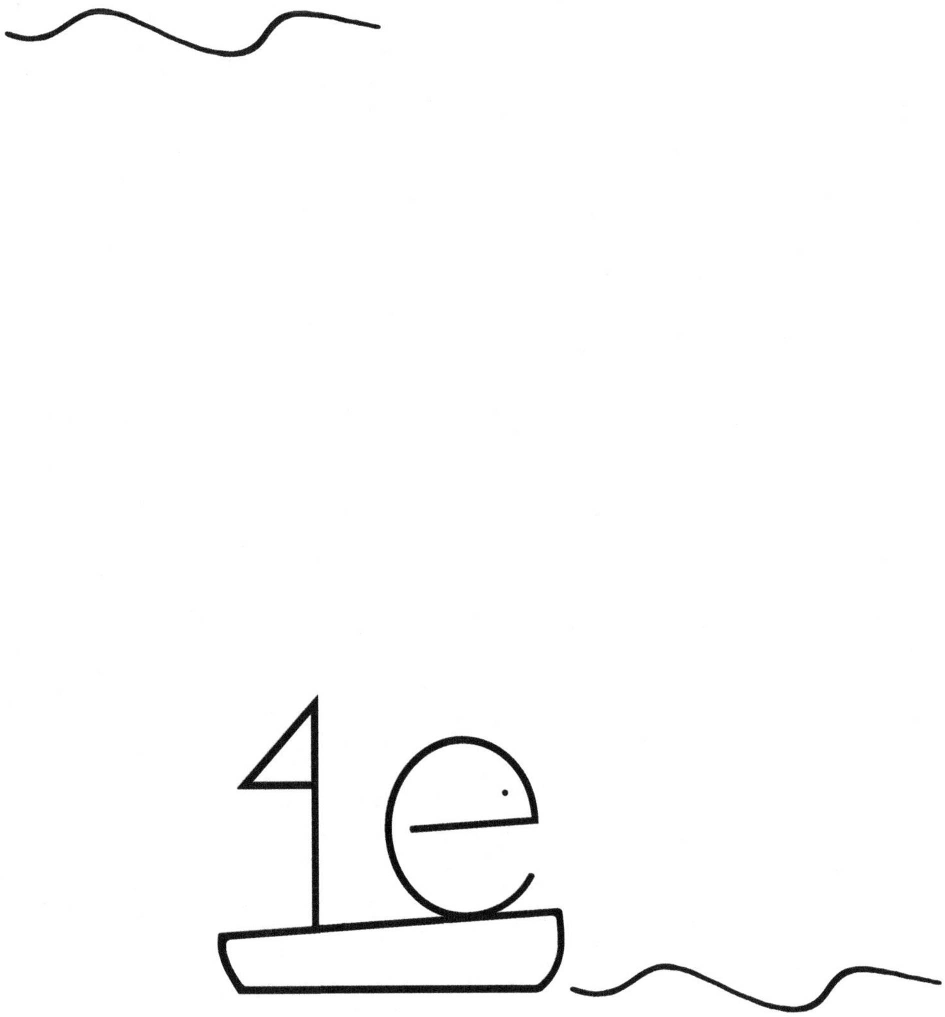

Restless yet hopeful it went on its way,

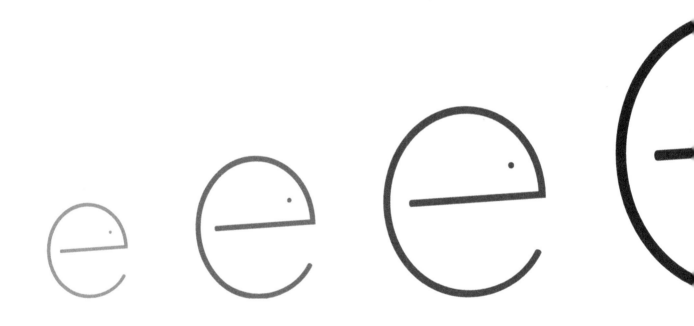

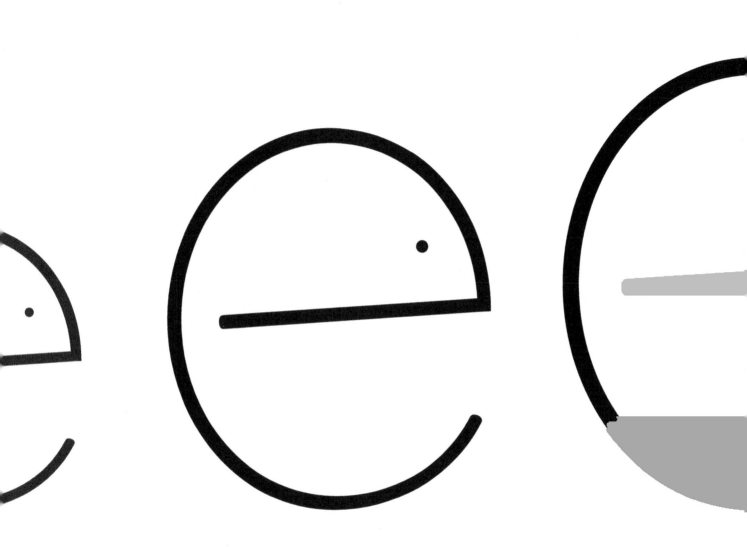

in search of some kind of meaning.

Soon it found others that resembled
its kind,

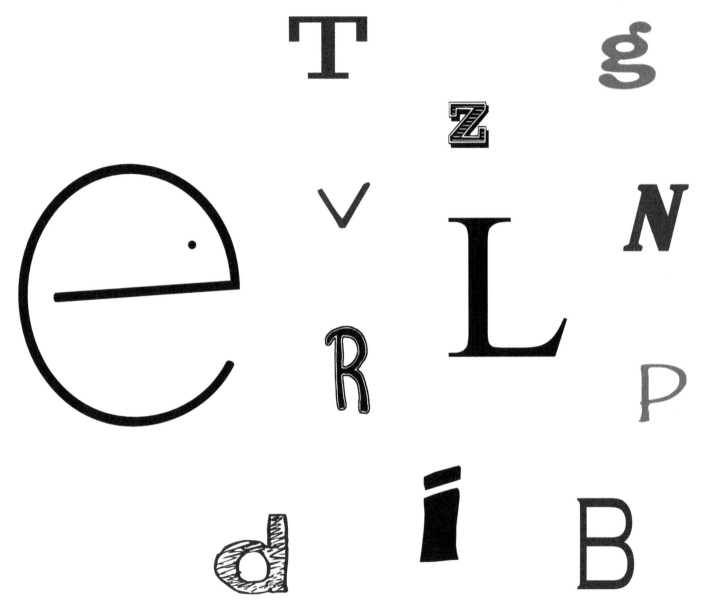

each with a vision and flare of its own.

Bewildered, determined and convinced there was more,

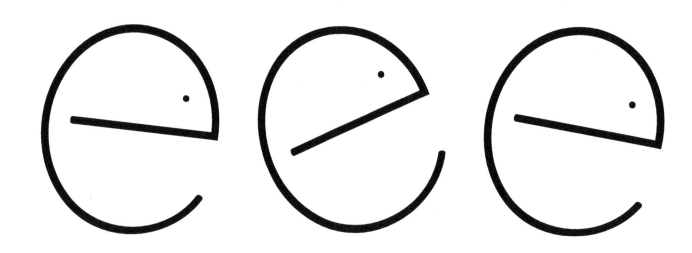

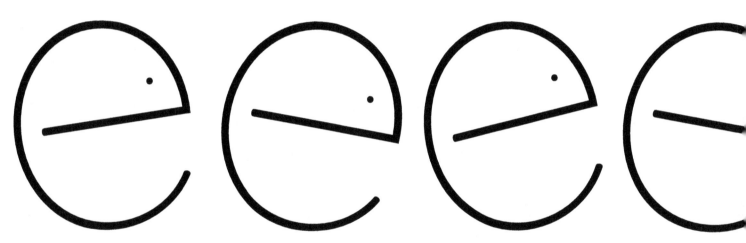

it marched on.

It came upon clusters that caused it to shrivel.

gossip

go away!

eNvY

SAD

different

Bro

PAIN

VICTIM

ken

BELITTLE

negative

FIGHT

alone

HURT

embarrass

I don't like you!

bad choices

GREED

ugly

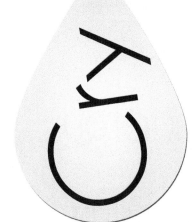
Cry

BULLY

Yet others that made it smile
and recover.

BeauTY

light

confidence

selfless

GOOD
choices

D

N

compassion

peace

KIND

energy

K

SELF-ESTEEM

Feelings

EMPOWER

friend

positive

RESPECT

Hugs

I care about you!

comfort

HAPPY

Let's Play

It bounced about from one to another,

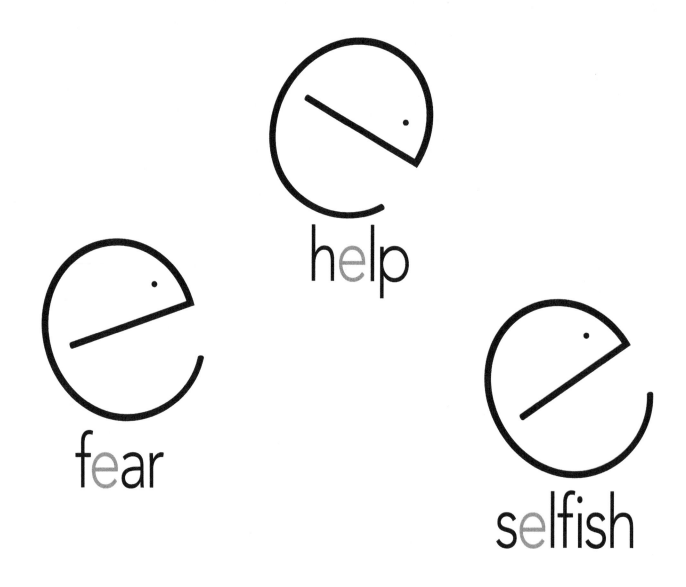

help

fear

selfish

smile

hope

mean

never quite finding a balance.

It glanced at the bold groups,
demanding and harsh -

CRUSHING

TAKING

DARING

It turned to the light ones,
inviting and mild -

inspiring

giving

sharing

It considered its options,

to build

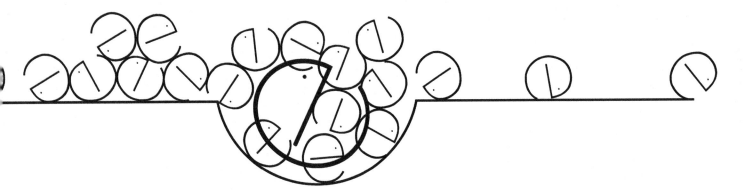

or destroy!

And decided ...

hat e

lov

there was ever only one choice -

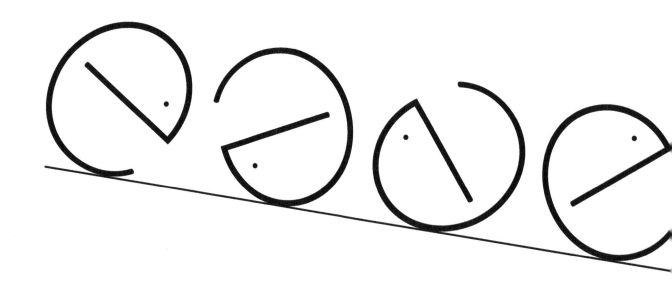

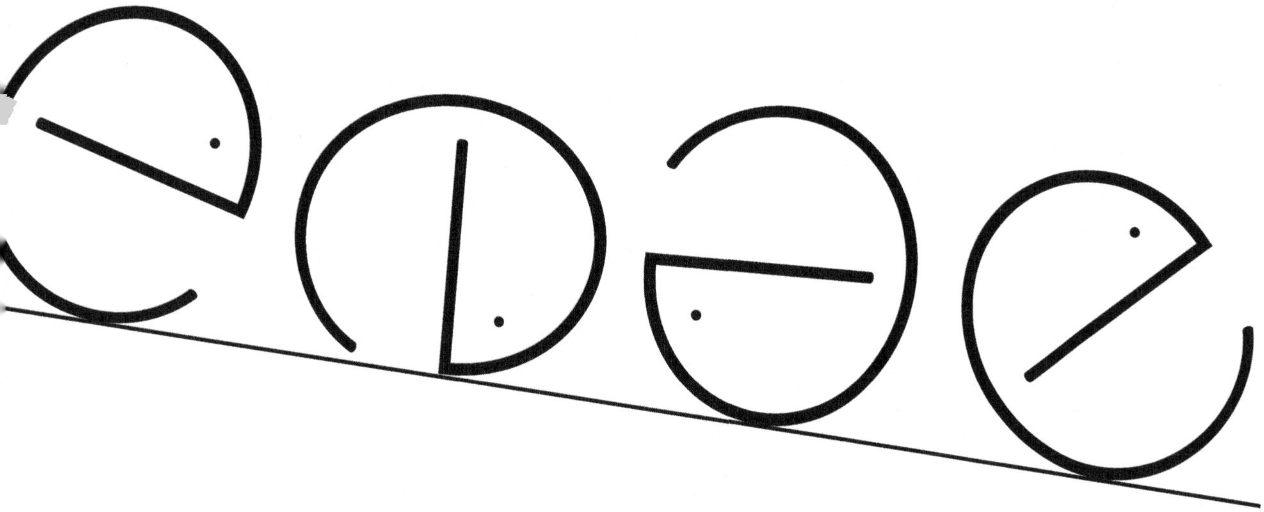

to

love!

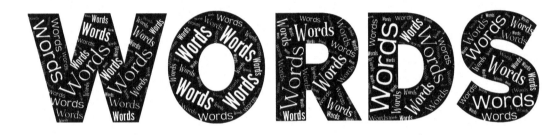

About the Author

Lora Rozler is an elementary school teacher whose passion for writing and art began at a young age. When she is not busy in the classroom or running around the vibrant city of Toronto, Canada, with her two children, she enjoys fiddling with words, crafting them into whimsical poems and stories.

To learn more, download resources and view an animated reading of Words, visit **lorarozler.com**.

CPSIA information can be obtained at www.ICGtesting.com
Printed in the USA
LVOW05s1614081015

457490LV00023B/64/P